SECOND PRINTING

Cover photograph by Robert Freeman

JOHN LENNON

A SPANIARD IN THE WORKS

SIMON AND SCHUSTER

New York

COPYRIGHT © 1965 JOHN LENNON

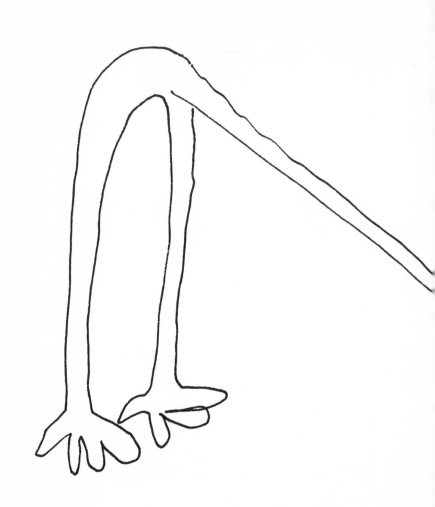

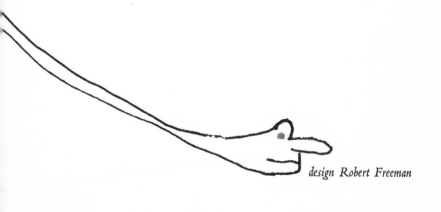

design Robert Freeman

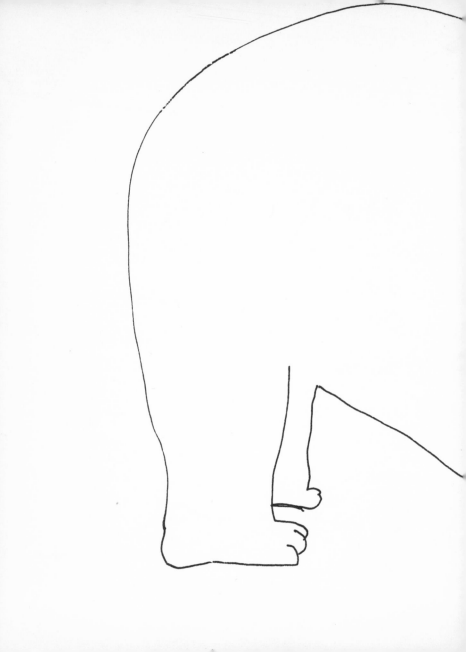

drawings John Lennon

CONTENTS

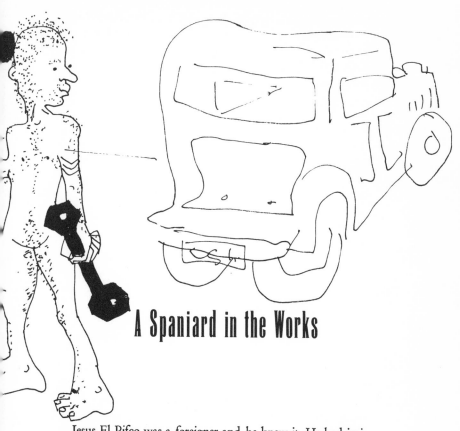

A Spaniard in the Works

Jesus El Pifco was a foreigner and he knew it. He had imi-grateful from his little white slum in Barcelover a good thirsty year ago having first secured the handy job as coachman in Scotland. The job was with the Laird of McAnus, a canny old tin whom have a castle in the Highlads. The first thing Jesus El Pifco noticed in early the days was that the Laird didn't seem to have a coach of any discription or even a coach house you know, much to his dismable. But – and I use the word lightly – the Laird did seem to having some horses, each one sporting a fine pair of legs. Jesus fell in love with them at first sight, as they did with him, which was lucky, because his quarters were in the actually stables along side his noble four lepered friends.

Pretty polly one could see Jesus almost every day, grooming his masters horses, brushing their manebits and hammering their teeth, whistling a quaint Spanish refrain dreaming of his loved wombs back home in their little white fascist bastard huts.

'A well pair of groomed horses I must say,' he would remark to wee Spastic Sporran the flighty chamberlain, whom he'd had his good eye on eversince Hogmanose.

'Nae sa bad' she would answer in her sliced Aberdeen martin accent. 'Ye spend more time wi' yon horses than ye do wi' me,' with that she would storm back to her duties, carefully tying her chastity negro hardly to her skim.

Being a good catholic, Jesus wiped the spit from his face and turned the other cheese – but she had gone leaving him once small in an agatha of christy.

'One dave she woll go too farther, and I woll leaf her' he said to his fave rave horse. Of course the horse didn't answer, because as you know they cannot speak, least of all to a garlic eating, stinking, little yellow greasy fascist bastard catholic Spaniard. They soon made it up howevans and Jesus and wee Spastic were once morphia unitely in a love that knew no suzie. The only thing that puzzled Jesus was why his sugarboot got so annoyed when he called her his little Spastic in public.

Little wonder howeapon, with her real name being Patrick, you see?

'Ye musna' call me Spastic whilst ma friends are here Jesus ma bonnie wee dwarf' she said irragated.

'But I cannot not say Patrick me little tartan bag' he replied all herb and angie inside. She looked down at him through a mass of naturally curly warts.

'But Spastic means a kind of cripple in English ma sweet wee Jesus, and ai'm no cripple as you well known!'

'That's true enough' said he 'but I didn't not realize being a foreigner and that, and also not knowing your countries culture and so force, and anywait I can spot a cripple anywhere.'

He rambled on as Patrick knelt down lovingly with tears in her eye and slowly bit a piece of his bum. Then lifting her face upwarts, she said with a voice full of emulsion 'Can ye heffer forgive me Jesus, can ye?' she slobbed. He looked at her strangely as if she were a strangely, then taking her slowly right foot he cried; 'Parreesy el pino a strevaro qui bueno el franco senatro!' which rugby transplanted means – 'Only if you've got green braces' – and fortunately she had.

They were married in the fallout, with the Lairds blessing of course, he also gave them a 'wee gifty' as he put it, which was a useful addition to their bottom lawyer. It was a special jar of secret ointment made by generators of his forefingers to help get rid of Patricks crabs which she had unluckily caught from the Laird of McAnus himself at his late wifes (Lady McAnus') wake. They were overjoyced, and grapenut abun and beyond the call of duty.

'The only little crawlie things we want are babies,' quipped Jesus who was a sport. 'That's right sweety' answered Patrick reaching for him with a knowsley hall.

'Guid luck to you and yours' shouted the Laird from the old wing.

'God bless you sir' said Jesus quickly harnessing his wife with a dexterity that only practice can perfect. 'Come on me beauty' he whispered as he rode his wife at a steady trot towards the East Gate. 'We mustn't miss the first race my dear.'

'Not likely' snorted his newly wed wife breaking into a gullup. 'Not likely' she repeated.

The honeymood was don short by a telephant from Mrs El Pifco (his mother) who was apparently leaving Barcelunder to see her eldest sod febore she died laughing, and besides the air would do her good she added. Patrick looked up from her nosebag and giggled.

'Don't joke about Mamma please if you donlang, she are all I have loft in the world and besides your mother's a bit of a brockwürst herselves' said Jesus, 'And if she's still alive when she gets here we can throw up a party for her and then she can meet all our ugly Scottish friends' he reflected. 'On the other handle we can always use her as a scarecrab in the top field' said Patrick practically.

So they packed their suitcrates marked 'his and hearse' and set off for their employers highly home in the highlies.

'We're home Sir' said Jesus to the wizened tartan figure knelt crouching over a bag of sheep.

'Why are ye bask so soon?' inquired the Laird, immediately recognizing his own staff through years of experience. 'I've had some bad jews from my Mammy – she's coming to seagull me, if its all ripe with you sir.' The Laird thought for a mumble, then his face lit up like a boiling wart.

'You're all fired' he smiled and went off whistling.

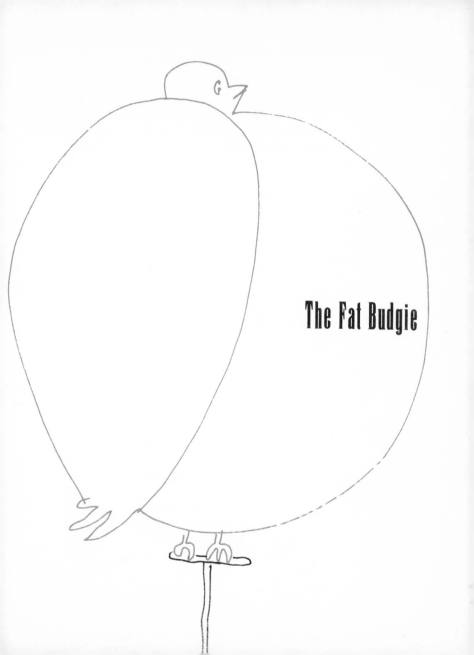

The Fat Budgie

I have a little budgie
He is my very pal
I take him walks in Britain
I hope I always shall.

I call my budgie Jeffrey
My grandads name's the same
I call him after grandad
Who had a feathered brain.

Some people don't like budgies
The little yellow brats
They eat them up for breakfast
Or give them to their cats.

My uncle ate a budgie
It was so fat and fair.
I cried and called him Ronnie
He didn't seem to care

Although his name was Arthur
It didn't mean a thing.
He went into a petshop
And ate up everything.

The doctors looked inside him,
To see what they could do,
But he had been too greedy
He died just like a zoo.

My Jeffrey chirps and twitters
When I walk into the room,
I make him scrambled egg on toast
And feed him with a spoon.

He sings like other budgies
But only when in trim
But most of all on Sunday
Thats when I plug him in.

He flies about the room sometimes
And sits upon my bed
And if he's really happy
He does it on my head.

He's on a diet now you know
From eating far too much
They say if he gets fatter
He'll have to wear a crutch.

It would be funny wouldn't it
A budgie on a stick
Imagine all the people
Laughing till they're sick.

So that's my budgie Jeffrey
Fat and yellow too
I love him more than daddie
And I'm only thirty two.

Snore Wife and some Several Dwarts

Once upon upon in a dizney far away – say three hundred year agoal if you like – there lived in a sneaky forest some several dwarts or cretins; all named – Sleezy, Grumpty, Sneeky, Dog, Smirkey, Alice? Derick – and Wimpey. Anyway they all dug about in a diamond mind, which was rich beyond compère. Every day when they came hulme from wirk, they would sing a song – just like ordinary wirkers – the song went something like – 'Yo ho! Yo ho! it's off to wirk we go!' – which is silly really considerable they were comeing hulme. (Perhaps ther was slight housework to be do.)

One day howitzer they (Dwarts) arrived home, at aprodes-tant six o'cloth, and who? – who do they find? – but only Snore Wife, asleep in Grumpty's bed. He didn't seem to mine. 'Sambody's been feeding *my* porrage!' screams Wimpey, who was wearing a light blue pullover. Meanwife in a grand Carstle, not so mile away, a womand is looging in her daily mirror, shouting, 'Mirror mirror on the wall, whom is de fairy in the land.' which doesn't even rhyme. 'Cassandle!' answers the mirror. 'Chrish O'Malley' studders the womand who appears to be a Queen or a witch or an acorn.

'She's talking to that mirror again farther?' says Misst Cradock, 'I've just seen her talking to that mirror again.' Father Cradock turns round slowly from the book he is eating and explains that it is just a face she is going through and they're all the same at that age. 'Well I don't like it one ti,' continhughs Misst Cradock. Father Cradock turns round slowly from the book he is eating, explaining that she doesn't have to like it, and promptly sets fire to his elephant. 'Sick to

22

death of this elephant I am,' he growls, 'sick to death of it eating like an elephant all over the place.'

Suddenly bark at the Several Dwarts home, Snore Wife has became a *firm favourite*, especially with her helping arm, brushing away the little droppings. 'Good old Snore Wife!' thee all sage, 'Good old Snore Wife is our fave rave.' 'And I like you tooth!' rejoices Snore Wife, 'I like you all my little dwarts.' Without warping they hear a soddy voice continuallykhan shoubing and screeging about apples for sale. 'New apples for old!' says the above hearing voice. 'Try these nice new apples for chris- sake!' Grumpy turnips quick and answers shooting – 'Why?' and they all look at him.

A few daisy lately the same voice comes hooting aboon the apples for sale with a rarther more firm aproach saying 'These apples are definitely for sale.' Snore Wife, who by this time is curiously aroused, stick her heads through the window. Anyway she bought one – which didn't help the trade gap at all. Little diggerydoo that it was parsened with deathly arsen- ickers. The woman (who was the wickered Queen in disgust) cackled away to her carstle in the hills larfing fit to bust.

Anyway the handsome Prince who was really Misst Cradock, found out and promptly ate the Wicked Queen and smashed up the mirror. After he had done this he journeyed to the house of the Several Dwarts and began to live with them. He refused to marry Snore Wife on account of his health, what with her being poissoned and that, but they came to an agreement much to the disgust of Sleepy – Grumpy – Sneeky – Dog – Smirkey – Alice? – Derick and Wimpy. The Dwarts clubbed together and didn't buy a new mirror, but always sang a happy song. They all livered happily ever aretor until they died – which somebody of them did naturally enough.

The Singu  large Experience

of Miss Anne Duffield

I find it recornered in my nosebook that it was a dokey and winnie dave towart the end of Marge in the ear of our Loaf 1892 in Much Bladder, a city off the North Wold. Shamrock Womlbs had receeded a telephart whilst we sat at our lunch eating. He made no remark but the matter ran down his head, for he stud in front of the fire with a thoughtfowl face, smirking his pile, and casting an occasional gland at the massage. Quite sydney without warping he turd upod me with a miscarriage twinkle in his isle.

'Ellifitzgerrald my dear Whopper,' he grimmond then sharply 'Guess whom has broken out of jail Whopper?' My mind immediately recoughed all the caramels that had recently escaped or escaped from Wormy Scabs.

'Eric Morley?' I ventured. He shook his bed. 'Oxo Whitney?' I queered, he knotted in the infirmary. 'Rygo Hargraves?' I winston agreably.

'No, my dear Whopper, it's OXO WHITNEY' he bel⁄lowed as if I was in another room, and I wasn't.

'How d'you know Womlbs?' I whispered excretely.

'Harrybellafonte, my dear Whopper.' At that precise mor, man a tall rather angularce tall thin man knocked on the door. 'By all accounts that must be he, Whopper.' I marvelled at his acute osbert lancaster.

'How on urge do you know Womlbs' I asped, revealing my bad armchair.

'Eliphantitus my deaf Whopper' he baggage knocking out his pip on his large leather leg. In warped the favourite Oxo Whitney none the worse for worms.

'I'm an escaped primrose Mr Womlbs' he grate darting franetically about the room.

'Calm down Mr Whitney!' I interpolled 'or you'll have a nervous breadvan.'

'You must be Doctored Whopper' he pharted. My friend was starving at Whitney with a strange hook on his eager face, that tightening of the lips, that quiver of the nostriches and constapation of the heavy tufted brows which I knew so well.

'Gorra ciggie Oxo' said Womlbs quickly. I looked at my colledge, hoping for some clue as to the reason for this sodden outboard, he gave me no sign except a slight movement of his good leg as he kicked Oxo Whitney to the floor. 'Gorra ciggie Oxo' he reapeted almouth hysterically.

'What on urn are you doing my dear Womlbs' I imply; 'nay I besiege you, stop lest you do this poor wretch an injury!'

'Shut yer face yer blubbering owld get' screamed Womlbs like a man fermented, and laid into Mr Whitney something powerful nat. This wasn't not the Shamrock Womlbs I used to nose, I thought puzzled and hearn at this suddy change in my old friend.

Mary Atkins pruned herselves in the mirrage, running her hand wantanly through her large blond hair. Her tight dress was cut low revealingly three or four blackheads, carefully scrubbed on her chess. She addled the final touches to her makeup and fixed her teeth firmly in her head. 'He's going to want me tonight' she thought and pictured his hamsome black curly face and jaundice. She looked at her clocks impatiently and went to the window, then leapt into her favorite armchurch, picking up the paper she glassed at the headlines. 'MORE NEGOES IN THE CONGO' it read, and there was, but it was the Stop Press which corked her eye. 'JACK THE NIPPLE STRIKE AGAIN.' She went cold all over, it was Sydnees and he'd left the door open.

'Hello lover' he said slapping her on the butter.

'Oh you did give me a start Sydnees' she shrieked laughing arf arfily.

'I always do my love' he replied jumping on all fours. She joined him and they galloffed quickly downstairs into a har-rased cab. 'Follow that calf' yelped Sydnees pointing a rude fingure.

'White hole mate!' said the scabbie.

'Why are we bellowing that card Sydnees?' inquired Mary fashionably.

'He might know where the party' explained Sydnees.

'Oh I see' said Mary looking up at him as if to say.

The journey parssed pleasantly enough with Sydnees and Mary pointing out places of interest to the scab driver; such as Buckinghell Parcel, the Horses of Parliamint, the Chasing of the Guards. One place of particularge interest was the Statue of Eric in Picanniny Surplass.

'They say that if you stand there long enough you'll meet a friend' said Sydnees knowingly, 'that's if your not run over.'

'God Save the Queens' shouted the scabbie as they passed the

Parcel for maybe the fourth time.

'Jack the Nipple' said Womlbs puffing deeply on his wife, 'is not only a vicious murderer but a sex meany of the lowest orgy.' Then my steamed collic relit his pig and walkered to the windy of his famous flat in Bugger St in London where it all hap/ pened. I pondled on his statemouth for a mormon then turding sharply I said. 'But how do you know Womlbs?'

'Alibabba my dead Whopper, I have seen the film' I knew him toby right for I had only read the comic.

That evenig we had an unexpeckled visitor, Inspectre Basil, I knew him by his tell/tale unicorn.

'Ah Inspectre Basil mon cher amie' said Womlbs spotting him at once. 'What brings you to our humble rich establisment?'

'I come on behave of thousands' the Inspectre said sitting quietly on his operation.

'I feel I know why you are here Basil' said Womlbs eyeing he leg. 'It's about Jock the Cripple is it not?' The Inspectre smiled smiling.

'How did you guess?' I inquired all puzzle.

'Alecguiness my deep Whopper, the mud on the Inspectre's left, and also the buttock on his waistbox is misting.'

The Inspectre looked astoundagast and fidgeted nervously from one fat to the other. 'You neville sieze to amass me Mr Womlbs.'

'A drink genitalmen' I ventured, 'before we get down to the businose in hand in hand?' They both knotted in egremont and I went to the cocky cabinet. 'What would you prepare Basil, Bordom '83 or?'

'I'd rather have rather have rather' said the Inspectre who was a gourmless. After a drink and a few sam leeches Womlbs got up and paced the floor up and down up and down pacing.

'Why are you pacing the floor up and down up and down pacing dear Womlbs' I inquiet.

'I'm thinking alowed my deaf Whopper.' I looked over at the Inspectre and knew that he couldn't hear him either.

'Guess who's out of jail Mr Womlbs' the Inspectre said subbenly. Womlbs looked at me knowingly.

'Eric Morley?' I asked, they shook their heaths. 'Oxo Whitney?' I quart, again they shoot their heaps. 'Rygo Hargraves?' I wimpied.

'No my dear Whopper, OXO WHITNEY!' shouted Womlbs leaping to his foot. I looked at him admiring this great man all the morphia.

Meanwire in a ghasly lit street in Chelthea, a darkly clocked man with a fearful weapon, creeped about serging for revenge on the women of the streets for giving him the dreadfoot V.D. (Valentine Dyall). 'I'll kill them all womb by womb' he muffled between scenes. He was like a black shadow or negro on that dumb foggy night as he furtively looked for his neck victim. His minds wandered back to his childhook, remembering a vague thing or two like his mother and farmer and how they had beaten him for eating his sister. 'I'm demented' he said checking his dictionary, 'I should bean at home on a knife like these.' He turned into a dim darky and spotted a light.

Mary Atkins pruned herselves in the mirrage running her hand wantanly through her large blond hair. Her tight dress was cut low revealingly three or four *more* blackheads carefully scrubbed on her chess. Business had been bad lately and what with the cost of limping. She hurriedly tucked in her gooseberries and opened the door. 'No wonder business is bad' she remarked as she caught size of her hump in the hall mirror.

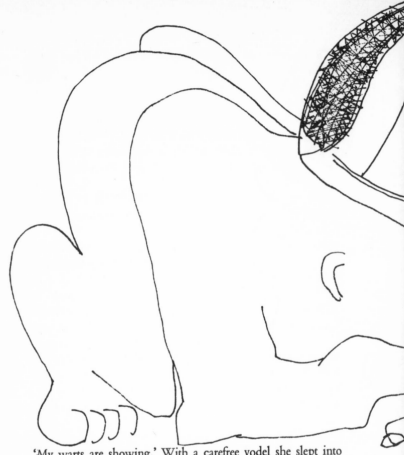

'My warts are showing.' With a carefree yodel she slept into the street and caught a cab to her happy humping grounds. 'That Sydnees's nothing but a pimple living on me thus' she thought 'lazing about day in day off, and here's me plowing my train up and down like Soft Arthur and you know how soft Arthur.' She got off as uterus at Nats Café and took up her

position. 'They'll never even see me in this fog' she muttered switching on her lamps. Just then a blasted Policemat walked by. 'Blasted Policemat' she shouted, but luckily he was deaf. 'Blasted deaf Policemat' she shouted. 'Why don't yer gerra job!'

Little did she gnome that the infamous Jack the Nipple was

only a few street away. 'I hope that blasted Jack the Nipple isn't only a few streets away,' she said, 'he's not right in the heads.'

'How much lady' a voice shocked her from the doorways of Nats. Lucky for him there was a sale on so they soon retched an agreament. A very high class genderman she thought as they walked quickly together down the now famous Carringto Average.

'I tell yer she whore a good woman Mr Womlbs sir' said Sydnees Aspinall.

'I quite believe you Mr Asterpoll, after all you knew her better than me and dear old buddy friend Whopper, but we are not here to discuss her merits good or otherwives, we are here, Mr Asronaute, to discover as much information as we can about the unfortunate and untidy death of Mary Atkins.' Womlbs looked the man in the face effortlessly.

'The name's Aspinall guvnor' said the wretched man.

'I'm deleware of your name Mr Astracan.' Womlbs said looking as if he was going to smash him.

'Well as long as you know,' said Aspinall wishing he'd gone to Safely Safely Sunday Trip. Womlbs took down the entrails from Aspinall as quickly as he could, I could see that they weren't on the same waveleg.

'The thing that puddles me Womlbs,' I said when we were alone, 'is what happened to Oxo Whitney?' Womlbs looged at me intently, I could see that great mind was thinking as his tufted eyepencil knit toboggen, his strong jew jutted out, his nosepack flared, and the limes on his fourheads wrinkled.

'That's a question Whopper.' he said and I marveled at his grammer. Next day Womlbs was up at the crack of dorchester, he didn't evening look at the moaning papers. As yewtree I fixed his breakfat of bogard, a gottle of geer, a slice of jewish bread, three eggs with little liars on, two rashes of bacon, a bowel of Rice Krustchovs, a fresh grapeful, mushrudes, some freed tomorrows, a basket of fruits, and a cup of teens.

'Breakfeet are ready' I showbody 'It's on the table.' But to my supplies he'd already gone. 'Blast the wicker basket yer grannie sleeps in.' I thought 'Only kidding Shamrock' I said remembering his habit of hiding in the cupboard.

That day was an anxious one for me as I waited for news of my dear friend, I became fretful and couldn't finish my Kennomeat, it wasn't like Shamrock to leave me here all by my own, lonely; without him I was at large. I rang up a few close itamate friends but they didn't know either, even Inspectre Basil didn't know, and if anybody should know, Inspectre Basil should 'cause he's a Police. I was a week lately when I saw him again and I was shocked by his apeerless, he was a dishovelled rock. 'My God Womlbs' I cried 'My God, what on earth have you been?'

'All in good time Whopper' he trousered. 'Wait till I get my breast back.'

I poked the fire and warmed his kippers, when he had minicoopered he told me a story which to this day I can't remember.

Softly softly, treads the Mungle
Thinner thorn behaviour street.
Whorg canteell whorth bee asbin?
Cam we so all complete,
With all our faulty bagnose?

The Mungle pilgriffs far awoy
Religeorge too thee worled.
Sam fells on the waysock-side
And somforbe on a gurled,
With all her faulty bagnose!

The Faul

agnose

Our Mungle speaks tonife at eight
He tell us wop to doo
And bless us cotten sods again
Oamnipple to our jew
(With all their faulty bagnose).

Bless our gurlished wramfeed
Me curséd café kname
And bless thee loaf he eating
With he golden teeth aflame
Give us OUR faulty bagnose!

Good Mungle blaith our meathalls
Woof mebble morn so green the wheel
Staggaboon undie some grapeload
To get a little feel
of my own faulty bagnose.

Its not OUR faulty bagnose now
Full lust and dirty hand
Whitehall the treble Mungle speak
We might as wealth be band
Including your faulty bagnose

Give us thisbe our daily tit
Good Mungle on yer travelled
A goat of many coloureds
Wiberneth all beneath unravelled
And not so MUCH OF YER FAULTY BAGNOSE!

We must not forget . . .

Azue orl gnome, Harassed Wilsod won the General Erection, with a very small marjorie over the Torchies. Thus pudding the Laboring Partly back into powell after a large abcess. This he could not have done withoutspan the barking of thee Trade Onions, heady by Frenk Cunnings (who noun has a SAFE SEAT in Nuneating thank you and Fronk (only 62) Bowels hasn't).

Sir Alice Doubtless Whom was – quote – 'bitherly ditha pointed' but managed to keep smirking on his 500,000 acre estate in Scotland with a bit of fishing and that.

The Torchies (now in apperition) have still the capable

. . . the General Erection

qualities of such disable men as Rabbit Bunloaf and the very late Harrods McMillion. What, you arsk, happened to Answerme Enos (ex Prim Minicar) after that Suez pudding, peaple are saying. Well I don't know.

We must not forget the great roles played out by Huge Foot and Dingie in capturing a vote or tomb. We must not forget Mrs Wilsod showing her toilets on telly. We must not forget Mr Caravans loving smile on Budgie Day as he raised the price of the Old Age Pests. We must not forget Mr Caravans lovely smile when he raised the price of the M.P.s (Mentals of Parliament) wagers as well also. We must not forget Joke Grimmace (LIB). We must not forget to issue clogs to all the G.P. Ostmen who are foing great things somewhere and also we must not forget to Post Early for Christsake.

Lastly but not priest, we must not forget to put the clocks back when we all get bombed. Harold.

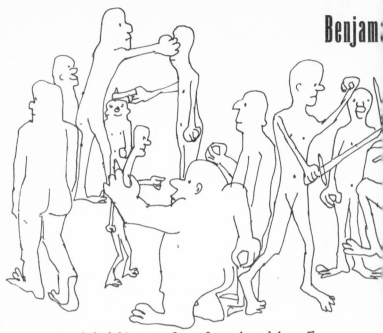

Benjaman halted his grave flow of speach and lug off a cigarf he knew where peeky boon! He wretched overy and berlin all the tootsdes.

'It were all nok a limpcheese then a work ferce bottle. Ai warp a grale regrowth on, withy boorly replenishamatsaty troop, and harlas a wedreally to fight. We're save King of pampices when all the worm here me aid.' I inadvertabably an unobtrusive neyber had looke round and seen a lot of goings off, you know how they are. Anywart, I say get a battlyard pussload, ye scrurry navvy, I beseige of all my bogglephart, way with his kind farleny and grevey cawlers. But Benjaman was a rather

man for all I cared. I eyed he looking, 'Ben' I cried 'You are rather man.' He looked at me hardly with a brown trowel. 'I know' he said, 'but I do a steady thirsty.' I were overwhelped with heem grate knowaldge, you darn't offer mead and monk with all these nobody, I thought. A man like he shall haff all the bodgy poodles in his hands. 'Curse ye baldy butters, and Ai think its a pritty poreshow when somebottle of my statue has to place yongslave on my deposite.'

'Why – why?' I cribble all tawdry in my best sydneys.

To this day I'll never know.

THE END

The Wumberlog (or The Magic Dog)

Whilst all the tow was sleepy
Crept a little boy from bed
To fained the wondrous peoble
Wot lived when they were dead.

He packed a little voucher
For his dinner 'neath a tree.
'Perhumps a tiny dwarf or two
Would share abite with me?

'Perchamp I'll see the Wumberlog
The highly feathered crow,
The larfing leaping Harristweed
And good old Uncle Joe.'

He packed he very trunkase,
Clean sockers for a week,
His book and denzil for his notes,
Then out the windy creep.

He met him friendly magic dog,
All black and curlew too,
Wot flew him fast in second class
To do wot he must do.

'I'll leave you now sir,' said the dog,
'But just before I go
I must advise you,' said his friend
'This boat to careflee row.'

'I thank you kindly friendly pal,
I will,' and so he did,
And floated down towards the land
Where all the secrets hid.

What larfs aplenty did he larf,
It seeming so absurd;
Whilst losing all his oars,
On his head he found a bird.

'Hello,' the bird said, larfing too,
'I hope you don't mind me,
I've come to guide you here on in,
In case you're lost at sea.'

Well fancy that, the boy thought,
I never knew till now
That birds could speak so plainly.
He wondered – wonder how?

'What kind of bird are you sir?'
He said with due respect,
'I hope I'm not too nosey
But I didn't not expect.'

'I am a wumberlog you see,'
The bird replied – all coy,
'The highly feathered species lad,
You ought to jump for joy.'

'I would I would, if only, but
You see – well – yes, oh dear,
The thing is dear old Wumberlog
I'm petrefried with fear!'

'Now don't be silly' said the bird,
'I friendly – always – and
I'm not like Thorpy Grumphlap,
I'll show you when we land.'

And soon the land came interview,
A 'tastic sight for sure,
An island with an eye to see
To guide you into shore.

'Hard to starboard' said a tree,
'Yer focsle mainsle blast
Shivver timbers wayard wind
At last yer've come at last.'

'You weren't expecting me, I hope'
The boy said, puzzled now.
'Of course we are' a thing said,
Looking slightly like a cow.

'We've got the kettle going lad,'
A cheerful apple say,
'I'll bring a bag of friends along
Wot you can have for tay.'

A teawell ate, with dog and tree
Is not a common sight,
Especially when the dog himself
Had started off the flight.

'How did you get here curlew friend?'
The boy said all a maze.
'The same way you did, in a boat,'
The dog yelled through the haze.

'Where are all the peoble, please,
Wot live when they are dead?
I'd like to see them if I may
Before I'm back in bed.'

'You'll see them son,' a carrot said,
'Don't hurry us; you know
You've got to eat a plate of me
Before we let you go!'

Then off to see the peoble whom
The lad had come to see
And in the distance there he saw
A group of twelve or three.

A little further on at last
There were a lot or more,
All digging in the ground and that,
All digging in the floor.

'What are you digging all the time?'
He asked them like a brother.
Before they answered he could see
They really dug each other.

In fact they took it turns apiece
To lay down in the ground
And shove the soil upon the heads
Of all their friends around.

Well, what a sight! I ask you now.
He had to larf out loud.
Before he knew what happened
He'd gathered quite a crowed.

Without a word, and spades on high,
They all dug deep and low,
And placed the boy into a hole
Next to his Uncle Joe.

'I told you not to come out here,'
His uncle said, all sad.
'I had to Uncle,' said the boy.'
'You're all the friend I had.'

With just their heads above the ground
They bade a fond goodbye,
With all the people shouting out
'Heres mud into your eye!'
(And there certainly was.)

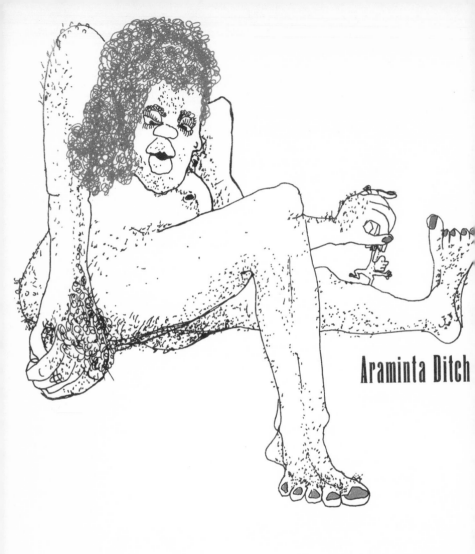

Araminta Ditch

Araminta Ditch was always larfing. She woof larf at these, larf at thas. Always larfing she was. Many body peofle woof look atat her saying, 'Why does that Araminta Ditch keep larfing?' They could never understamp why she was ever larfing about the place. 'I hope she's not at all larfing at me,' some peokle would say, 'I certainly hope that Araminta Ditch is not larfing at me.'

One date Araminta rose up out of her duffle bed, larfing as usual with that insage larf peojle had come to know her form.

'Hee! hee! hee!' She larfed all the way down to breakfart.

'Hee! hee! hee!' She gurgled over the morman papiers.

'Hee! hee! hee!' Continude Araminta on the buzz to wirk.

This pubbled the passages and condoctor equally both. 'Why is that boot larfing all the time?' Inqueered an elderberry passengeorge who trabelled regularge on that roof and had a write to know.

'I bet nobody knows why I am always larfing.' Said Araminta to herself privately, to herself. 'They would dearly love to know why I am always larfing like this to myselve privately to myselve. I bet some peoble would really like to know.' She was right, off course, lots of peotle would.

Araminta Ditch had a boyfred who could never see the joke. 'As long as she's happy,' he said. He was a good man. 'Pray tell me, Araminta, why is it that you larf so readily. Yeaye, but I am sorly troubled sometimes when thy larfter causes sitch tribulation and embarrement amongst my family and elders.' Araminta would larf all the more at an outburp like this, even to the point of hysteriffs. 'Hee! hee! hee!' She would scream as if possesed by the very double himself.

'That Araminta Ditch will have to storp orl these larfing; she will definitely have to storp it. I will go crazy if she don't storp it.' This was the large voice of her goodly neighbore, Mrs Cramsby, who lived right next door and looked after the cats whilst Araminta was at work. 'Takes a good deal of looking after these cat when she's at work – and that's nothing to larf about!'

The whole street had beginning to worry about Araminta's larfter. Why? hadn't she been larfing and living there for nye bevan thirty years, continually larfing hee! hee! and annoying them? They began to hold meters to see what could be done – after all they had to live with her hadn't they? It was them who had to always keep hearing her inane larftor. At one such meetinge they deciple to call on the help of Aramintas' boyfiend who was called Richard (sometimes Richard the Turd, but thats another story). 'Well I dont know dear friends,' said Richard, who hated them all. This was at the second meetink!

Obvouslieg samting hed tow be doon – and quickly.

Aramintas' face was spreading aboon the country, peochle fram all walks of leg began to regarden her with a certain insight left.

'What canon I do that would quell this mirth what is gradually drying me to drink, have I not bespoken to her often, betting her to cease, threatling – cajolson – arsking, pleases stop this larftor Araminta. I am at the end of my leather – my cup kenneth conner,' Richard say. The people of the street mubbered in agreement, what could he do? He was foing his vest. 'We will ask the Vicar,' said Mrs Crambsey, 'Surely he can exercise it out of her?' The peodle agreed – 'Surely the Vicar can do it if anybotty can.' The Vicar smiled a funny little smile wholst the goo people splained the troumer. When they had had finished speaching he rose up grandly from his barthchair and said loud and clear 'What do you mean exactly?' The peodle sighed an slowlies started to start again telling him about the awful case of Araminta's larfing.

'You mean she just keeps larfing fer no a parent season?' he said brightly. 'Yess that's it fazackerly Vicar,' said Richard, 'morning noon and nige, always larfing like a mad thin.' The Vicar looked up from his knitting and opened his mouths.

'Something will have to be done about that girl larfing all the time. It's not right.'

'I really doughnut see that it is any concervative of thiers whether i larf or nament,' sighed Araminta over a lengthy victim. 'The trifle with the peomle around here is that they have forgoden how, I repeat, how to larf, reverend, that's what I think anyhow.'

She was of corset talking to the extremely reverend LIONEL HUGHES. She had gone to see him in case he could help her in any small way, considering he was always spouting off about helping peouple she thought she'd give him a try as it were. 'What can I say my dear, I mean what can I say?' Araminta looked at the holy fink with disbelief. 'What do you mean – what can I say – don't ask me what to say. I cam here to ask you for help and you have the audacidacidity to ask me what to say – is that all you have to say?' she yellowed. 'I know exactly how you feel Samantha, I had a cousin the same way, couldn't see a thin   without his glasgows.'

Araminta stood up in a kind of suit, she picked up her own mongels and ran seriously out of the room. 'No wonder he only gets three in on Sunday!' she exclaimed to a small group of wellwishers.

A year or more passedover with no changei in Araminta's strange larfing. 'Hee! hee! hee!' she went drivan herself and everone around her insane. THERE SEEMED NO END TO THE PROBLEM. This went on for eighty years until Araminta died larfing. This did not help her neighbers much. They had all died first, – which was one of the many things that Araminta died larfing off.

CASSANDLE

You all know me

How many times have I warned you all about my telephone? Well it happened again! *Once more I couldn't get through to my Aunty Besst, and yet again I nearly didn't get my famous column with a picture of me inset through those damn blasted operators!* YOU know how I hate those damn blasted operators. You all know me. THIRTY TWO times I tried to get through with my famous column and thirty two times I was told to 'Gerroff the line yer borein' owld gassbag!' When I told a colleague or two, they couldn't not believe it, after all hadn't I been writing the same thing for sixty years? You all know me . . .

The way I see it

How many moron of these incredible sleasy backward, bad, deaf monkeys, parsing as entertainers, with thier FLOPTOPPED hair, falling about the place like Mary PICKFORD, do I have to put up with? *The* way I see it, a good smell in the Army would cure them, get rid of a few more capitalist barskets (OOPS!). Not being able to stand capitalism, I fail to see why those awful common lads make all that money, in spite of me and the government in a society such as ours where our talent will out.

I know I'm a bald old get with glasses (SEE PICTURE). *Maybe I ought to be thankfull, but I doubt it . . .*

Koms der revolution

Caviar is collected for me with Hollywood. Do you remember when I had dinner with that super spiffing showdog Mike 9 (Round the Wall in Eighty Days, the late) Toddy? Well he loved caviarse/great pots of it/ and he assulmed derry boddy elf did and if they didn't, they should, damn it (OPPS!). *You* all know me, well I don't like it, and I find myself (somtimes) fighting a fierce and wonderfull verbal battle as to whether I should be forthed against *my* will to eat this *costly* delicasy from the Caspian Sea. Quite orften I lose, but thats Socialism. (*You know me*).

Mike (Round the Worst in A Tall Canoe, the late) Toddy would have liked me.

I suppose a lot of you have never had the chance of refusing this costly delicacy, believe me fans, you never will if we keep building all those bombs . . .

Until tomorrow friends when I (YOU ALL KNOW ME) will be back with the same picture, but a DIFFERENT QUOTE brothers.

Good Day, (The way I see it!)

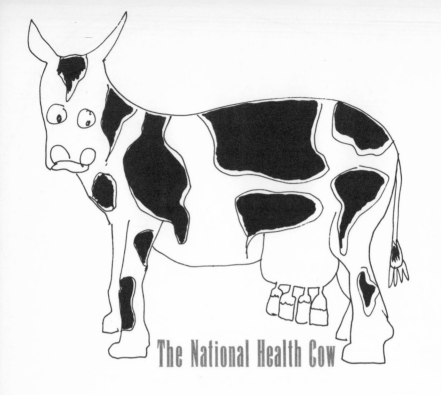

The National Health Cow

I strolled into a farmyard
When no-one was about
Treading past the troubles
I raised my head to shout.

'Come out the Cow with glasses,'
I called and rolled my eye.
It ambled up toward me,
I milked it with a sigh.

'You're just in time' the cow said,
Its eyes were all aglaze,
'I'm feeling like an elephant,
I aren't been milked for days.'

'Why is this?' I asked it,
Tugging at its throttles.
'I don't know why, perhaps it's 'cause
MY milk comes out in bottles.'

'That's handy for the government,'
I thought, and in a tick
The cow fell dead all sudden
(*I'd smashed it with a brick*).

Readers Lettuce

Dear Sir,

IF Mr Mothballs (Feb, 23 Sun'Taimes, page 8. col 4), thinks that the Hon gentleman (Norman Ccough). Well I'm here to tell him (Mr Mothballs) that he has bitten off more than he can chew. How dearie imply that Mr Ccough is socially inpurdent? Was it not Ccough whom started off the worled wide organiseationses, which in turn brought imidiate response from the Western Alliance (T.U.R.). If Mr Smith-barbs sincerely imagines that Indonegro is really going to attack the Australian continent with the eyes of the worled upon them I can only asulme that he (Mr Smallburns) has taken leaf of his sentries! Has he forgetting Mr Ccough's graet speek at the Asembly of Natives? Is he also forbett-ing that hithertoe unpressydessy charter- the Blested Old Widows - which was carried through the House with a Majollity vote?

In future I hobe thet Mr Smellbarth will refrian frog makeing wild and dangeroo statemonths.

Iremain still,

yours for the arsking,

Jennifarse Cough (no relations).

P.S. CAN I HEVE A PHOTY OF WINDY STANDSTILL?

Editors Football.

Well maa'mm, the old Coblers think you're a very plucky christion. Wish there were a few more like yourself maa'mm!!!!

Silly Norman

'I really don't know woot tow mak of these.' said Norman, as he sorted through him Chrimbas posed. 'It seem woot I git mower litters und parskels than woot I know peoples, it suplizeses moi moor et moor each yar, as moor on these pareskle keep cooming. I really doon't knaw whew all they body are – seddling ik all this.' He clab quitely too the fire, sheving a few mough ruddish awn. 'It's came tow a pretty parse when I don't evil knew where they cam frog.' Norman coop an stetty keel and prumptly wed intow thee kitcheon tow put up thee kettle

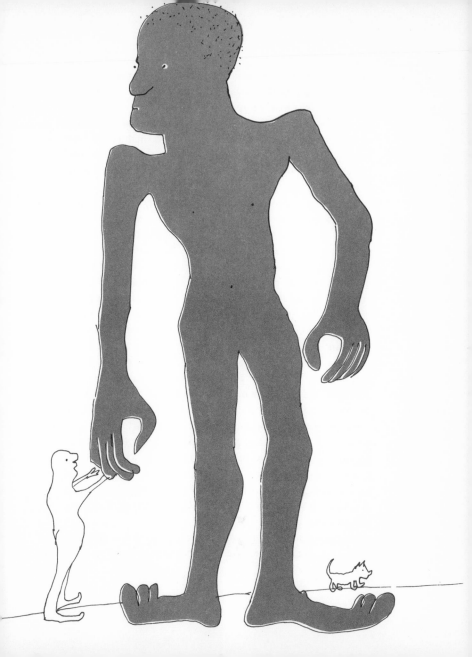

orn. 'I might as welsh mak me a cooper tea, I night as welp hev a chocolush birskit as well, wile I do noddy.' So saying so he marshed offer to that teapod and tap it to that sing: bud to he grey suffise – what! – bat noo warty. 'Goob heralds! what's all of thiz goinge awn? Doe mein ice desleeve me? Am I knot loofing at me owen sing⁄unice, and there be know warty?' He was quait raight, lo! the warty didn noo apear, trey as he maybe.

Off course we all know whey this warty do no coomb, becourgh the tangs they are awl freezup, awl on they, awl they freezop. Norman dig knort know that, for Norman him a silly man – yes – Norman is sorft. 'OH deally meat! oh woe isme, wart canada, ther are nay werters toe mick a caper tay, ange me moover she arther cooming ferty too. I shall heave two gough nextador, perhats they might hall hefty.' Sow Norman he gentry poots his had hand coat orn makeing sewer to wrave hisself op like he moomy tell him, broosh beyond the ears and out of that frant door he ghost. To him truly amasemaid, he fainds nought a houfe nought a hough inside! Wart on earth is heffer⁄ing? – why – there iznot a hug tobeseen, not anyway fer miles aboot. 'Goody Griff, which artery in HEFFER harold be thy norm! is these not thet enid of the worm? Surely to goosestep I am nit that larst man on earn?' he fell suddy to the ground weefy and whaley crizeling tuber Lawn aboove to savfre him or judge spare a friend or to. 'I wilf give of awl my wordy posesions, awl me foren stabs, awl me classicow rechords, awl me fave rave pidgeons of Humpty Littlesod thee great nothing. All these oh wondrouse Sailor up above, I offer ye if only yer will save me!'

Normans mather, who you remembrane, was a combing tooty, was shorked when she cam acroose him lyinge awn the floor thus crying. 'My dear NORMAN!' she screege, 'Wart in Griffs' nave are you doing, why are you carroling on this way?' She wogged slightly over to her own son, with a woddied loof in her eye. 'Police don't garryon like this my son, tell Muddle werts the metre.' Norman raved himself slowly and sabbly locked at her. 'Carrot you see, mubber, Griff have end the worled. I only went to guess sam warty, and then it dibble wirk, so I went to go necktie to a nebough and I saw wit had happened – GRIFF had ended the worl. I saw nothing – every where there where no neybers. Oh Mather wet is hap⁄ pening?' Normans mither take won loog at he with a disabe⁄ leafed spression on her head. 'My Golf! Norman wit are yuo torking about turn? Donald you member thet there have been nobodys livfing here ever? Remelble whensday first move in how you say – "Thank Heavy there are no peoplre about this place, I want to be aloef?" have you fergit all thistle?' Norman lucked op at he mam (stikl cryling) with teeth in his eye, saying – 'Muther, thou art the one, the power ov atterny, for heavan sakes amen. Thank you dear mether, I had truly forgot. I am a silly Norman!' They booth link arbs and walk brightly to the house.

'Fancy me ferbetting that no⁄bottle lives roynd here mother! Fantasie forgetting thet!' They each laff together as they head four the kitchenn – and lo! – that warty runs again, the sunbeefs had done it, and they booth have tea, booth on them. Which jub shaw yer – –

> 'However blackpool tower maybe,
> In time they'll bassaway.
> Have faith and trumpand B B C –
> Griffs' light make bright your day.'
> AMEN (and mickaela dentist.)

69

Mr. Boris Morris

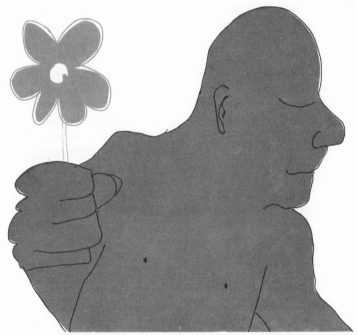

However Mr Boris Morris was morgan thankful for his narrow escape is largely put down to his happy knack of being in the right place at the right place. For stance, Boris was the one whom cornered Miss Pearl Staines at her impromtu but lighthearted garbage partly.

'Miss Staines' he had shouted 'how come you never invited yer sister to the do?'

'For the same reason I didn't invite you Mr Morris' she replight reaching for anoven helping.

Boris was no fudge, he quickly melted into the backcloth like an old cake, slighly taking candy shots of Miss Staines with her relatively.

'She won't invite me to the next do either' he remarked out loud with above average clarity.

Boris was elsie the man whom got the photies of the Dupe of Bedpan doing things at the anyearly jap festival, much to the supper of the Duchess set. Thus then was Boris Morris a man of great reknown and familiarity, accepted at do's of the wealthy and the poor alike hell. He was knew as the jew with a view, and he had. Not long after one of his more well known esca-pades, he was unfortunable to recieve a terrible blow to his ego. He was shot in the face at a Hunt Ball but nobody peaple found out till the end becaugh they all thought it was a clever mask.

'What a clever mask that man has on,' was heard once or twig.

It was not the end of Boris as you might well imargin, but even before his face set he was to easily recognizable at most places, with peaple pointing at him saying thing like 'What a good shot' and other. All this set Boris thinking, specially in the morning when he was shaving his scabs, as only he knew how.

'Must fix this blob of mine' he'd smile over a faceful of blotting paper.

'You certainly must dear' said his amiable old wife, 'what with me not getting any younger.'

71

Bernice's Sheep

This night I lable down to sleep
With hefty heart and much saddened
With all the bubbles of the world
Bratting my boulders
Oh dear sheep

I slapter counting one be one
Till I can cow nomore this day
Till bethny hard aches leave we
Elbing my ethbreeds
Dear Griff's son

What keeps me alberts owl felloon
That is earl I ask from anybottly
That I grape me daily work
Cronching our batter
My own bassoon.

Can I get a gribble of me
Should I heffer alway sickened
Should you nabbie my furbern
Wilfing their busbie
Oh dear me.

No! I shall streze my eber-teap!
With lightly loaf and great larfter
With head held eye and all
Graffing my rhimber
Oh dear sheep.

Last Will and Testicle

'I, Barrold Reginald Bunker-Harquart
being of sound mind you, limp and bodie,
do on this day the 18 of Septemper 1924th,
leave all my belodgings estate and brown
suits to my nice neice Elsie. The above
afformentioned hereafter to be kept in a
large box untit she is 21 of age, then to be
released amongst a birthdave party given
in her honour. She will then be wheeled
gladly into the Great Hall or kitchen,
and all my worldly good heaped upon her
in abundance. Thus accordian to my word
will this be carried out as I lie in the
ground getting eaten.'

This then was the last will and testicle of I Barrold Reginald Bunker-Harquart, which was to change the lives of so many peoble – speciality little Elsie whom was only thirteens.

'Are you sure I have to stay in the box?' asked Elsie childishly.

'Yer not deaf are yer?' yelled Freud Q.C. what was helping. 'Yer 'eard the familias solister as good as we didn't yer?'

'I was only makeing conversation' replied Elisie who was only thirteen.

Just then Elisies dear Old Nanny Harriette broke down in tears and everybody walked quietly out of the room leaving her to her grease, except Dr (not the) Barnado.

'There there Harriette, that won't bring the Mastered back' he said knowingly.

'I know I know' she bluttered 'its not that, its where are we going to find a box to fit *her* foot? tell me that, where are we going to find a box to fit *her* foot?' Luckily the Dr knew a carpentor in the village who was A WONDER WITH WOOD. 'I'm a wonder with wood.' he used to say, as he sored his way through life – with a nail in one hand and polio in the other (his light hand being stronger than his lest). 'Children should be seized and not hard' was something Uncle Barrold had always said and *even* Old Nanny had always replied 'Overy clown has a silver lifeboat' which always dried him ap.

Anywait, Elisie was soon entombed in her made to marion box, and people from miles adavies would come and visit HER, but only when it was sunny – for she was kept rightly in the garden. 'At least she'll get some fresh air.' argued Old Nanny – and she was right.

Three years parst and a great change had come over Elsie.

Her once lovely skin was now roof and ready, some say it was that last bitter winter, others say it wasn't. Her warm smile which made one forget her hairlip was now a sickly grin, but enough of that.

Less and lessless people came to visit Elsie especially since Old Nanny had put the price up. The Dr had kindly devised a scheme whereby Elsie could call for anything she wanted. It was a primitive affair, but effective – just a simple microphone tied into Elsie's mouth. This was attached to a louder speaker in the kitchen. Of course when Old Nanny was away on holiday, she would turn the speaker off. 'No point in her shouting if I'm away' she would explain.

The years flew by for Elsie in her own box, sooner no than it was coming round to her twenty-first burly. 'I hope I get the key of the door' she thought, forgetting for a moment she was getting the whole house. The place was was certainly in a state of anticipatient on the ear of Elsie's birthdaft, and Old Nanny celebrated by bringing her into the house for 'a warm by the fire' as she put it. Unfortunately Old Nanny seemed to place birthday Elsie too near the big old fireplace and her box caught alight with Elsie still wrapped firmly inside like her Uncle asked.

'She didn't even eat her cake,' said Old Nanny tearfulham to Dr (not the) Bernardo the next morning.

'Never mind' he wryled. 'we'll give it the dog, he'll eat anything.'

With that the Dr leap'ed over and gave Old Nanny a thorough examination on her brand new carpet.

'You can't have your cake and eat it' said a cheerful paying guessed adding, 'S atistics state that 90% of more accidents are caused by burning children in the house.'

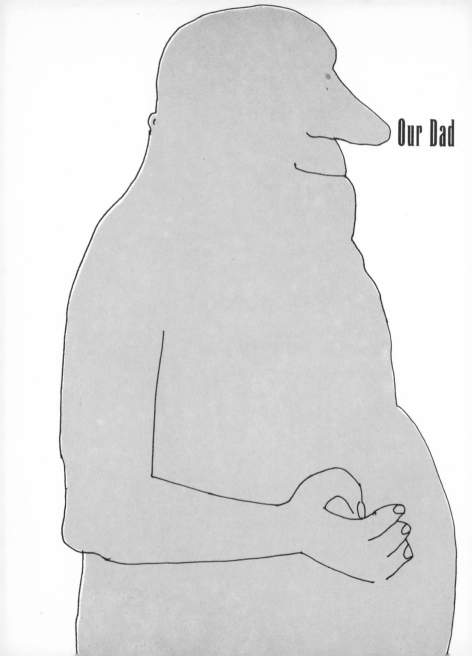

Our Dad

It wasn't long before old dad
Was cumbersome – a drag.
He seemed to get the message and
Began to pack his bag.

'You don't want me around,' he said,
'I'm old and crippled too.'
We didn't have the heart to say
'You're bloody right it's true.'

He really took an age and more
To pack his tatty kleid.
We started coughing by the door,
To hurry him outside.

'I'm no use to man nor beast,'
He said, his eye all wet.
'That's why we're getting rid of you,
Yer stupid bastard, get.'

His wrinkled face turned up to us
A pleading in his look;
We gave him half-a-crown apiece
And polished up his hook.

'Its not that we don't like you dad.'
Our eyes were downcast down.
'We've tried to make a go of it
Yer shrivelled little clown!'

At last he finished packing all,
His iron hand as well. ·
He even packed the penis
What he'd won at bagatell.

''Spect you'll write a line or two?'
He whined – who could resist?
We held his face beneath the light
And wrote a shopping list.

'Goodbye my sons and fare thee well,
I blame yer not yer see,
It's all yer mothers doing lads,
She's had it in for me.'

'You leave our mother out of this!'
We screamed all fury rage,
'At least she's working for her keep
And nearly twice your age!'

'I'd sooner starve than be a whore!'
The old man said, all hurt.
'Immoral earnings aren't for me,
and living off her dirt.'

'She washes everyday,' we said
Together, all at once.
'It's more than can be said for you
Yer dirty little ponce!'

At last upon the doorstep front
He turned and with a wave
He wished us all 'Good Heavens'
And hoped we'd all behave.

'The best of luck to you old dad!'
We said with slight remorse,
'You'll dig it in the workhouse man.
(He wouldn't though of course.)

'Ah well he's gone and thats a fact,'
We muttered after lunch,
And hurried to the room in which
He used to wash his hunch.

'Well here's a blessing in disguise;
Not only money too;
He's left his pension book as well
The slimy little jew!'

'What luck we'll have a party
Inviting all our friend.
We've only one but she's a laugh
She lets us all attend.'

We never heard from dad again
I 'spect we never shall
But he'll remain in all our hearts
– a buddy friend and pal.

Aman came up to me the other day and said – 'Tell me
vicar – tell me the deafinition of sin?' – and you know, I
couldn't answer him! Which makes me think – do you ever
wonder (and what do we mean by the word wonder?) what
an ordinary man (and what – I ask myself do we mean by
an ordinary man?) who works in office or factory – goes
to church on Sunday (what exactly do we mean by
Sunday?) who is also a sinner (we are all sinners).
People are always coming up to me and asking – 'Why, if
Griff is so good and almighty – why does he bring such
misery into the world?' – and I can truthfully say St. Alf – ch
8 verse 5 – page 9. 'Griff walks in such mysterious ways
His woodwork to perform' (what do we mean by perform?)
Which leads me neatly, I feel, to our next guest for tonight –
A man whom is stickle trodding the pathway to our beloved
Griff – slowly but slowly I am here to help with the bridges he
must surely crooss. – 'Welcome to our studios tonight Mr
Wabooba (a foreigner)'

Mr W. 'Hellow you Rev boy.'

Rev.   Well! Mr Wobooba – may I call you Wog? What is
         the basic problem you are facing? (He smiles)

Mr W. 'You! white trash christian boy.' (He also smiles)

Rev.   Hmn! can you hallucinate? (He colours)

Mr W. 'I can.' (Colouring too)

Rev.   Well? (He smiles)

Mr W. 'Wot ah want to know man – is why almighty Griff
         continooally insists on straiking ma fellow blackpool
         inde fayse?'

Rev. A man travelling on a train – like you or I – to
Scotland, had two or two bad eggs in his pocket –
and you know – no one would sit by him.

Mr W. 'But ah dont see dat yo' christship. Ah mean, ah don't
see de relevence.'

Rev. Well, Wabooba – let me put it this way. In Griff's
eye, we are all a bunch of bananas – swaying in the
breeze – waiting as it were, Wabooba – to be peeled
by His great andunderstanding love – some of them
fall on stonycroft – and some fall on the waistcoat.

Mr W. 'Well yo' worship, ah says dat if de Griff don't laike
de peoples in de world starfing an' all dat c'n you tell
me why dat de Pope have all dem rich robesan'
jewelry an big house to live – when ma people could
fit too tousand or mo' in dat Vatican Hall – and also
de Arch bitter of Canterbubble – him too!'

Rev. Ai don't think that the Arch bishoff would like to live
in the Vatican with that many people Mr Wabooba
– besides he's C. of E.

Mr W. 'Ah don't mean dat you white trash christmas imperialist!'

Rev. No one has ever called ME an imperialist before,
Mr Wabooba. (He smiles)

Mr W. 'Well ah have.' (Smiling too)

Rev. You certainly have Mr Wabooba.

90

(He turns
other chin and leans forward slowly looking at Mr
Wabooba rather hard. Mr Wabooba leans forward
rather more quickly and they both kiss.)

Mr W. 'Ah forgive you in de name of Fatty Waller de great
savious of ma people.' (He smiles)

Rev.   Ai too am capable of compassion dear Wabooba –
and in the name of the Fahter, Sock and Micky
Most, I forgive you sweet brother.
(With that they clasp each other in a brotherly way
as if forgetting they are still on camera.)

Rev.   Have you ever been to Brighton dear Watooba?

Mr W. 'Ah jes' got back sweet christian friend non de worse
for wearing.' (They get up glassy eyed and linking arms
slowly walk out of the studio to the very left proving
that arbitration is one answer to de prodlem.)
FADE OUT ON SUITABLE CHRISTIAN
CAPTIONS

The End